All Women Love Chocolate

"A Guide to Dating & Relationships"

About the Author

Kareem is a graduate of Michigan State University, graduating in 1995 earning a Bachelor's of Natural Science degree in Physiology and a minor is Spanish Language and Culture. In 1998, he returned to his Spartan Alma Mata and earned a Masters of Physiology.

His strong faith in God and dedication to ministry led him to be licensed as a Minister in 1998 by the late Bishop Marvin C. Pryor of Victorious Believers Ministries (VBM). During his 25-year tenure at VBM he served in several leadership capacities, before being ordained an Elder in 2005.

Elder Bowen continues his work with professional sports athletes as a Sports Entertainment Manager and Marketing Director. He has had the opportunity to work with some of the best players in the league; building brands and establishing players as marketable entities.

In December 2013, Elder Bowen founded The Potter's Touch International Ministries with just 7 members. Since then, God has grown the ministry to over to include: over 200 members with international members in Budapest, Switzerland, Germany;

ministry partnerships with churches in Kenya, Uganda, and Pakistan, SVSU Impact Campus Ministry servicing over 400 students, and a daily inspirational video blog, "Morning Manna with Pastor K".

Pastor Bowen has evolved his personal ministry to include Inspirational Speaker, Life Coach, Author "Reclaiming a Lost Generation".

His life motto is derived from Proverb's 16:3, "Commit your work unto the Lord and your thoughts will be established."

Table of Contents

INTRODUCTION

THE SCIENCE BEHIND THE CRAVINGS

THE CHOCOLATE BAR PROFILES

WHAT DOES YOUR MAN'S PROFILE MEAN?

Your Man should not only make you *FEEL AMAZING*, he should make You *BE AMAZING*!

INTRODUCTION

The adage exclaims that *"diamonds are a girl's best friend"*. Women around the world dream of the moment when their knight in shining armor kneels on one knee and asks their hand in marriage, presenting them with that bling of their affection. Clarity, Cut, and Carats are the three most important "C's" of many women's adult lives. Now please understand me! I'm not trying to say that every woman is desperate for wedding nuptials, however; it is the single most desired occasion (aside from giving birth) that women long to experience.

I mentioned that there are 3 important C's in a woman's life. Actually, there are four: clarity, cut, carats, and CHOCOLATE! You might be saying to yourself, "Boy, bye!" However, preceding the childhood dreams of fairytales and Prince Charming, young girls first crush is often this smooth, dark, sweet confection. Before 'puppy love' there was chocolate; before the occurrence of the "monthly visitor", there was chocolate. It plays an important role in every girl's life. When dad leaves and Johnny breaks your heart; It's safe, sweet, and always available.

A woman's love for chocolate can range from a casual affair to the ultimate declaration that chocolate is better than sex!

Researchers have found that chocolate is hands down the number one food women crave. Dark Chocolate, White Chocolate, Milk Chocolate, and all of its associations from Cookies 'N Cream to Chocolate and Peanut Butter; women have set their affections on this delightfully tasty super food!

All Women Love Chocolate is an informative guide for women who love chocolate, but have come to realize that chocolate doesn't always love them. For many women, it adds extra weight, blotches their skin, causes mood swings, and can even lead to addictive behaviors that are sinister and severely dangerous to their well-being.

I'm not pushing a tell-all of the games that men play, but rather a guide for women to reference while navigating the peaks and pitfalls of dating and relationships.

Included are *The Chocolate Profiles*; a collection of characteristics associated with each chocolate bar. Due to a need for brevity, I could not include every profile that exists, but I profiled the strongest examples that exist. When you're in a relationship you're too close and have too much time and emotion invested to really see it for what it truly is.

It is my prayer that women who are in negative relationships will be able to see themselves and their significant others in the pages of this book. Also, I have a selfish interest in writing this expose as well. I'm tired of being attracted to what seems to be an amazing woman, only to find, after further interaction, that she has been fractured beneath the surface from the "*Imitation chocolate*" before me.

Love and lust have a way of blinding and deafening us to sound judgment. However, when we see others crazy over-the-top relationships, it is much easier to recognize what you would not have been able to see in your own.
Fact is, everybody's played the fool at some point in our lives.

This book will challenge you to examine the kind of men you attract, are attracted to, and may shed some light on how you've become a "serial dater"; dating the same type of man repeatedly, just a different name.

It is important to understand that there is great truth in the law of attraction. What you attract is often an indication of what you put out! Pay attention to the bait you've been using

.

JUST REMEMBER, YOU CATCH WHAT YOU BAIT FOR!

Chocolate is delicious, but it can also be dangerous! Certainly, by now you've arrived at the understanding that I'm not just talking about sweets. No, not at all. In this discussion, *CHOCOLATE* is a metaphor for the men you love.

The Science Behind the Cravings…

To understand why *All Women Love Chocolate*, it is helpful to understand the chemistry behind the craving. In an effort to inform you and not bore you, I kept it short and sweet.

Chocolate is powerful! It triggers neurotransmitters and hormones, which are responsible for emotional responses, feelings of comfort, joy, and sensuality.

Following are a listing of the key transmitters and hormones and their associated effects:

- ***Theobromine***: A caffeine-like stimulant that perks you up.

- ***Tryptophan***: Increases the brain's serotonin levels for a happy, feel-good result.

- ***Serotonin***: Many women experience lowered serotonin levels in the 7 to 10 days prior to their menstrual cycles, which is one reason why premenstrual women often have powerful cravings for chocolate.

High levels of stress can also make women and men crave chocolate, since increasing serotonin levels can also lead to significant reductions in anxiety. Chocolate is a popular comfort food. It is the leading choice by emotional eaters. It can raise serotonin levels and helps "*comfort eaters*" forget about emotional or other problems, low self-esteem or a mildly depressed mood.

- ***Phenethylamine***: Releases endorphins, causing feelings of passion and love.

- ***Oxytocin***: It is known as "The Love and Trust Hormone" because your brain releases it every time you hug someone or a stranger holds the door open for you. **"Oxytocin"** is the connection between sex, friendship, maternal instinct and trust in strangers.

The Spiritual Significance...

In addition to science there is also a spiritual significance...

We never take the time to consider that relationships are as much spiritual as they are physical and emotional. God created women with three very distinct parts: body, soul, and spirit. A great part of why we often choose the wrong mate is because we make our decision solely on the first two parts of our physical existence, body and soul, and we neglect the spirit.

You were created a spiritual being. If you are to be pleasing to him, you must do so taking full account of the needs of your spirit-woman. Just as our nations governmental laws govern our cities and communities; spiritual laws govern our lives. We don't see them posted in courtrooms and placards on the roads, but they are the underlying factors that truly determine when we've met the right one.

Sex and relationships are more intricately interwoven in your God-relationship than most people could ever imagine.
When a woman has sex with a man, it is as much a spiritual connection, as it is physical. It's the physical and emotional experience that you remember (the sweat, the intensity, the

mental stimulation, and the smells), but it's the spiritual experience (the fact that your spirit becomes intimately connected) that lingers with you and governs your life.

When the passionate pleasures of a sexual escapade are over, you physically get out of bed, but a piece of your spirit is forever tied to that man that you allowed to ravish your body.
He's not only made love to your body, but was authorized to make love to your spirit. This is why it's so hard to get over some men whom you've allowed to enter that sacred space which was reserved for your husband, your life-mate. You develop a spiritual desire to have him near you, around you, inside of you. This is the result of spiritual intimacy.

Zebras all look alike, even to other zebras. When a mother has a new colt. She stands in front of him so that the first image it sees is its' mother's markings. Those markings are imprinted in the colt's mind and it will never confuse another zebra with his mother. She is mentally embellished in the young colt's mind. This is called imprinting. When a man has sex with a woman, he imprints on her. She bears a spiritual connection to that man. Because sex was designed to be enjoyed in the confines of the marriage union.

You try to understand why you have difficulties in dating and relationships; but you fail to understand that you can't move forward in a new relationship, because you're still connected to the ones of your past. You're bound from future relationships because you have soul ties that repel men from you. (Soul ties is a topic we'll cover in a future edition)

God created you to be a one-man woman. His divine plan was for you to find one man that could satisfy your every waking urge and desire; for him to love you with Godly intention as your prophet, priest, and king. Many men are of the opinion, the more women they satisfy, the greater their manhood. But the truth is, the greatest feat of a man is if he can satisfy one woman, forever.

> *Then the Lord God said to the woman, "What is this you have done?" The woman said, "The serpent deceived me, and I ate." So, the Lord God said to the serpent, "Because you have done this, "Cursed are you above all livestock and all wild animals! You will crawl on your belly and you will eat dust all the days of your life. And I will*

*put enmity between you and the woman and between your offspring and hers; he will crush your head and you will strike his heel." To the woman he said, "I will make your pains in childbearing very severe; with painful labor you will give birth to children. **<u>Your desire will be for your husband</u>**, and he will rule over you." – Genesis 3:13-16 KJB version*

Most women don't realize that their desire to be connected to a man is a desire that was divinely created. After man's transgression in The Garden of Eden, there was a longing placed in women to yearn after her perfect mate, that special piece of confection that she can call her own. All women love chocolate because The Creator above designed it to be so.

How can such a Heavenly treat that was divinely inspired, become the biggest agent of so much hell?

The Chocolate Bar Profiles
Just the Basics

1. THE TWIX

As of 2014, the slogan for Twix candy bars is "Try both and pick a side." The ad campaign is based on a fictional origin story of Twix that claims two Victorian inventors created the candy, but fought constantly until each made his own factory for the Twix Bars.

The TWIX is the guy who enjoys playing games with your mind. He is often controlling, intimidating, and on occasion loses control. That's right ladies, he's the kind of brother that will beat you down like a red-headed step child and 30 minutes later tell you it was a mistake; he's sorry, and it will never happen again. He will shower you with more affection than your heart can enjoy in one serving. Many women find themselves in love with The Twix because at first his extreme attention to the details of your life. He makes you feel special that he's so concerned and interested in knowing you inside and out.

Remember that a Twix has two sides to him; a dualistic personality. The public will often be convinced by his warm personality that he is sweet as honey, but be not deceived, if you are in love with or dating a Twix you will eventually get a taste of the bitter with the sweet. The honeymoon phase of this relationship may last extended periods of time, even years. In relationships, he is a public success and private failure; charming with the friends and family and short and even silent with you.

It's impossible to fathom that beneath the smooth milk chocolate surface lies a flaky cookie until you've completely engaged with your teeth fully submerged.

This relationship will leave you feeling emotionally, mentally and physically immobile. This toxic relationship is one in which you and your partner have an extreme attraction to one another, but have such drastically different morals, opinions, or integrity that all you do is fight. You bring out the worst in each other, but you can't stay away from each other. You're always on edge in this relationship. It's like being on a drug: the highs are very high, but the lows leave you incapacitated. The two never seem to be able to come together. If you are in a relationship with a TWIX, you must understand that a double minded man is unstable in all his ways.

He is very volatile and will often cause you to feel like a bunny trapped in a box. Friendships are challenged, family ties become strained and all your attention is diverted to stroking the ego of the maniacal Twix.

Being in a relationship with him is dangerous and may land you in the hospital on several occasions or worse, a permanent trip to the mortuary. Beware of the Twix....

Have you ever dated a Twix? If so, write his/their names below:

_____

How did you meet this individual?

_____

_____

_____

_____

How did you feel in this relationship?

The beginning: _____

_____

_____

The end: _____

_____

_____

Share 3 things you learned about yourself in this relationship?

1. _____

2. _____

3. _____

Were you ever physically harmed? If so, how?

_____

_____

_____

Have you healed from this relationship? Have you been able to move to a space in your heart that you no longer blame yourself, have forgiven him, and can move forward in a meaningful, emotionally healthy relationship, if so, how?

_____

_____

2. THE KIT KAT

"Break me off a piece of that Kit Kat bar"

The Kit Kat is a chocolate-covered wafer biscuit bar paneled into four bars, which can easily be broken off into four equal bars.

As the jingle of the candy bar suggests, the Kit Kat is not interested in a committed relationship. Ladies who desire to be "wifey" to him can throw in the towel because he offers a relationship that is met by an unusual dynamic of sex with no commitment.

Though at first earshot it sounds ludicrous and unthinkable, there are millions of women who have been pleasure-trapped in a lust-driven relationship with the Kit Kat bar.

Remember the Kit Kat bar is smooth and sweet on the outside which is the real essence of his appeal. He is usually overly good-looking, with chiseled abs, athletic build, radiant smile and very likable. Quite often he is the life of the party. He is often (or has been) an exotic dancer, male escort or a baller; some industry that thrives on the overproduction of testosterone. All the women want a piece of him and he's eager to oblige. He will sleep with best friends, sisters, even an occasional mother-daughter tandem if the opportunity presents itself. There is no emotional attachment to sex for him, so morality never enters the equation. Love and Sex are synonymous to him. In fact, Love = Sex.

The real secret to understanding his emotional disconnect lies in the mysteries of his childhood that in many cases was usually marked by a severe breakdown in parental nurturing and supervision.

This dude often has experienced first-hand the pain associated with growing up on his own and the often deficient of the bond that connects a mother to her son; coupled by the lack of appreciation for women that a father is responsible to instill in his sons.

He runs through women like toilet paper and jumps in-and-out of relationships like he changes his clothes. He uses them, wipes himself clean of them and flushes them away with no remorse or attachment. There's never any intimacy; cuddling nor foreplay. Everyone should know, "You don't squeeze the Charmin."

His knowledge of how to treat a woman was taught by men who never knew the value of a woman; most often by derelicts in the streets, pimps, pushers, and baby daddies who only see the value of a woman through the folds of her vagina.

If you are in love with a Kit Kat, call Dr. Phil immediately because you are positioned for a mental and/or an emotional breakdown.

Have you ever dated a Kit Kat? If so, write his/their names below:

_____

How did you meet this individual?

_____

_____

How did you feel in this relationship?

The beginning: _____

_____

_____

The end:

_____

_____

_____

How did this relationship eventually end?

_____

_____

_____

What did you sacrifice in this relationship?

_____

_____

What did you learn about your sexual appetite?

_____

_____

_____

3. THE ALMOND JOY

"Sometimes you feel like a nut, Sometimes you don't"

The relationship the Almond Joy offers is highly sexual accompanied by dysfunction. When you call or text one another, it's almost always to spend time *immediately.* You're mostly in the bedroom together. You have great sexual chemistry, and for some reason never feel compelled to explore your chemistry in other areas. This develops into a longer than expected term relationship where neither party knows how to end it. Lust is often mistaken for love. You don't get along or have very much in common, but you break up to make up, because the makeup sex is Heaven. All rhyme and reason are thrown out the window in this relationship.

He differs from the Kit Kat, because he really wants to be with you. In his mind the two of you are in a relationship with promise, but in your heart, you know you could never be with him because he doesn't stimulate your mind, nor does he understand what it takes to be in a relationship that would satisfy you.

He's the guy you love to see come and can't wait to see go. You love being around him and the way he makes you feel: sensual, womanly, desirable, even wanted; however, you wouldn't think of him meeting your friends and family. He's your *dirty little secret*.

Though these occasional romps in the chocolate factory leave you feeling like a kid in a candy store and seem harmless since both parties are consenting adults, they are very destructive to your mental and emotional psyche.

There is no real future with the Almond Joy. He's just good for sex, that's his value to society. He is some self-proclaimed ladies' man whose life's mission is to give women what their usual well-tailored suitors can't provide...unbridled passion.

The Almond Joy is particularly dangerous for "Fixers". Fixers are those women who believe they can fix what's wrong with a man. They attribute his issues to a lack of parental concern, support, nurturing as a child. The Fixer believes they have been a special "something" to rehabilitate their bad boys' naughty behavior. We will talk more about the perils of "the fixer" later in the book.

He doesn't necessarily come from a disturbed past, but he's never been challenged to evolve beyond his love for women.

He a nice guy with some good friends, but he lacks motivation, and that's a major turn off for you.

The Almond Joy is the guy that won't leave your home. You head to work and he heads to the fridge and then the couch to play the PS4 you bought him to keep him entertained while at YOUR home. When You return home from a hard day's work, he's right where You left him. On Your sofa playing video games and munching on the last of Your Dorito's.
Do you notice the trend here?

YOUR HOME
     YOUR JOB
          YOUR CAR
               YOUR MONEY
                    YOUR FRIDGE
                         YOUR A FOOL!

Oops! Did I just say that? Yep, and it's true. hopefully it's loud and clear.

I'm sure all of you have seen that scenario. You're at the pump of a gas station and a car pulls up. It's a semi-attractive young woman in the driver's seat. She gets out of the car, bends across the front seat and asks her companion what he wants from inside the store. She proceeds to make the purchases and returns with his bag of snacks, before returning to pump her gas. (He never lifts a finger except while he's texting – probably another female or his boys on his new I-Phone, which she also bought for him).

He has told you that he has an interest in you as a companion. You're not just a chic in his rotation, everyone knows better. If your man has a steady rotation of women that you know of and you're still around…You're a nut and he's an Almond Joy! "Sometimes you feel like a nut, sometimes you don't". You may feel like you're the "main chick" and those birds are just trying to get your man, but if you are continually having to "clap back" (respond) at other girls (or female cousins that you've never met) posts, tweets, and DM's on social media; face the facts, you're part of a rotation.

So, don't get upset when he leaves your company, and you go straight to vmail. Lol. He was so attentive to your physical needs while with you, but the moment you drop him off at his boys or "cousins house" (whom, again, you've never met) something goes wrong with his phone, he doesn't hear it because the ringer stops working properly. (ON HIS NEW I-PHONE…. that YOU bought him. Interesting. It was just working at the gas station. SMH!

You continually deal with the trauma packed, baby mama drama filled relationship, because he's good between the sheets and makes you feel pleasure you've never experience.

You know he's cheating. You've even talked to the other women on secrets calls whenever he falls asleep and you check his phone.

You send her slick-mouthed texts when he's with you, hoping she'll get the picture and just disappear; realizing that it's you he really wants.

She's sure to return the favor with pics of them together on social media at a family members get together.

Any man that will allow himself to be put on social media with another woman is NOT YOUR MAN!!! Ijs (I'm just saying)

The Almond Joy is good at what he does because he makes you believe that you'll never find another man that will be as attentive to your needs or love you like he does. The crazy thing is he believes it and if you aren't careful ladies…. you will to after a while.

ITS' TIME FOR AN INTERVENTION!!!

Until you realize the true value IN YOU, you'll wear the price tag that someone else places ON YOU.

Life with the Almond Joy is like a 90's R&B song. "Joy and Pain is like Sunshine and Rain". The craziest thing about this relationship is that you know he's not the one nor are you interested in having him full time. You just don't like losing or being alone, so you stay in the cycle.

Have you ever dated an Almond Joy? If so, write his/their names below:

_____

_____

_____

_____

_____

Where did you meet this individual?

_____

_____

How did you feel in this relationship?

The beginning:

_____

_____

_____

The end: _____

_____

_____

What actions did you take against the "other women" that were

a part of his rotation?

_____

_____

_____

Has your self esteem taken a blow? How do you feel about

yourself now? _____

_____

_____

_____

_____

_____

_____

_____

What caused you to stay as long as you did? _____

_____

_____

_____

_____ -

Until you realize the true value IN YOU, you'll wear the price tag that someone else places ON YOU.

4. THE MOUNDS
"INDESCRIBABLY DELICIOUS"

He is relaxing to be around and easygoing. He makes it easy to be around him, because he understands the stakes at hand and knows that he has them stacked in his favor. The taste of coconut and other exotic flavors appeal to him as he is well traveled. His life is filled with trips to world destination beaches, the lavish life, hammocks, and exotic drinks with little umbrellas in them. He is fun to be around and has a nice, breezy personality.

He may or may not be good-looking, but women date this guy because they're intrigued by what life is like on his arm. He regulars the best restaurants, drives the finest automobiles, a VIP on every socialite's guest list, and usually is looking for beautiful, young women to help him enjoy the spoils of his success.

He is quick to shower you with gifts from expensive boutique shops: Michael Kors, Louis Vuitton, Chanel, and Prada; with occasional trips to exclusive jewelers to put a little sparkle around your wrists. Ladies, I know exactly what you're thinking. This sounds like the guy of your dreams! Well, not exactly.

You see this guy realizes that his drawing power is his money, power, and/or his celebrity and he utilizes this tool to the point of great exploitation.

He knows that all women love chocolate, but also understands Jimmy Choo's and Prada handbags make great companions as well. He uses an expensive purse and shoe ensemble to say, "I'm sorry for cheating on you." Or buys you a nice piece of property to say, "I'm sorry, please take me back." He views buying you expensive gifts as a demonstration of his love; not realizing that real women would prefer a man who can make them a nice BLT and share the truth of his heart and the passions of his life.

If you're an emotionally sound woman, you typically can't carry this on for long. It's always nice to be showered with gifts, but you crave a real connection and this guy connects with his personal financial statement better than he does your emotions. Not to mention, the moment your actions don't please him he takes away his generosity as your punishment. This is why this guy is always surrounded by yes men and a flock of groupies on deck prepared to do anything and everything to be by his side.

The Mounds is actually attracted to and desires a woman who has substance, a career, family-oriented, strong-willed and focused. He knows that's the kind of women he actually needs in his life, but hasn't reached maturity to make the necessary lifestyle changes to acquire her. This requires the effort of "saying no to side chicks, baby mama's and jump offs".

Why in the world would he deal with the demands of fidelity and monogamy, when he has women (lurking in chat rooms and VIP lounges) who are okay with knowing they are one of many. So many women sacrifice their personal worth and become cool with it, as long as they get to live in the big house on a hill, attend the hottest functions on his arm, are afforded an occasional shopping spree?

The sad thing is that this guy actually wants the woman who challenges him, but ends up with the woman that lays down for him and pops out a kid or two.

He is the guy that just can't get over the fact that he can't have his cake and eat it too. Though he may marry the woman that he can run over, because she suffers from a complexity of esteem issues and a lack of personal value; he will always try to have the woman who excites his mind and challenges him to be better.

He will never be yours, because the other woman will do whatever she has to do to keep him. Unless you're willing to lower your personal self-worth to that of a side chick, you gotta let this brother go. He's a good guy, with a great personality, but he lacks a few characteristics that prevent him from being a great man: decisiveness, integrity, and commitment.

Ladies, if you're willing to sacrifice true love for the hope of a posh lifestyle, there will always be a mounds ready to buy you, but he will only place a value you that he sees, not your true value. Just remember, only prostitutes, hookers, and "garden tools" are willing to offer fleshy favors for finances.

Have you ever dated a Mounds? If so, write his/their names:

_____

Where did you meet this

individual?_____

_____

How did you feel in this relationship?

The beginning: _____

_____

_____

Do you think a man should pay your bills, take you on shopping sprees if you are intimate with him? Why?

_____

_____

_____

Do you think it's possible for a Mounds to change his playboy

ways?

_____

_____

_____

Do you think a well established, secure, woman with healthy

self esteem would accept this type of relationship?

_____

5. THE 3 MUSKETEER

Up to this point most of our profiles have been reflective of men with wandering eyes and attention spans of gnats, who requires great work to be tamed. This doesn't hold true for the 3 Musketeer.

He is more than willing to give you all his love and affection. In fact, he wants to be with you 24 hours 7 days a week and you wouldn't have it any other way.

The 3 Musketeer is that guy who knows how to get on your last nerve, but for some reason, you can't do without him. This strange-love relationship is a mystery to everyone around you, including yourself.

He's the guy that has a duffle bag full of issues that you so conveniently explain away to each and every one of your friends.

This relationship is the epitome of co-dependency. He gives you the time and attention that your previous "Almond Joy" never would; in exchange, you provide him with a pass for every single shortcoming and character flaw he exhibits.

He's extremely toxic but it's impossible for you to see things that way because he loves you the way no other man has taken an effort to do so.

If you're not sure if you've ever dated a 3 Musketeer, ask your friends. He's the one that all of your girlfriends had to plan an intervention, presented as a "girls' night out", just to get inside your head. The conversation probably started out about old times and how much fun everyone used to have then, seamlessly transitioned to your relationship. "Girl since you got with "Insert <u>3 Musketeer's name</u>" we never see you anymore. Why don't you have any time for your girls anymore?"

Initially, you thought their questions were carefully designed to pull you and "him" apart, but as time passed on you began to realize all the things you've compromised for the Musketeer's attention.

When he first approached you, there was ZERO interest. You said you'd never date a man with multiple baby mommas, a chronically unemployed man with bad credit or San Quinton's finest; but he kept coming. The flowers kept arriving, the flattering comments flowed like a river and gave you life!

Eventually, the "one date" you offered to get rid of him turns into six months later.

Ladies, I understand that when no one's checking for you and you run across a guy who makes you feel like the world revolves around you; giving you all his time and attention; it's easy to give him an "A" for effort.

WHEN THE NEED TO FEEL SECURE AND WANTED IS FULFILLED, WE WILL AMEND QUALIFYING STANDARDS THAT ARE NECESSARY, AND OFTEN MOST VITAL!

Co-dependent relationships are dangerous as we look for someone who is incomplete to complete areas that we are lacking in our lives.

Though Mr. Musketeer may make you feel amazing, does he make you better?

Any man that is in your life should not only make you feel amazing, but should make you BE AMAZING!

Have you ever dated a 3 Musketeer? If so, write his/their names below:

_____

How did he get through the front door?

_____

_____

_____

Take a good look in the mirror and ask yourself, "Am a running low on self esteem? Am I longing to feel the appreciation of a man? Be honest, what's your 1st response to these questions?

_____

_____

_____

_____

_____

6. THE REESE'S
"There's no wrong way to eat a Reese's."

The Reese's Peanut Butter Cup is smooth and consistent and comfortable, kind of like an old shoe. Women love shoes, and a cute pair of heels is always a must. However, when you know you have to be on your feet for an extended period of time, you always throw that one pair of flats in your bag that make your feet feel like you're walking on clouds. When your 'dogs get to barking' (that means when your feet start hurting for the less urban reader, lol) you can't wait to ditch the sexy pump for that old trusty, reliable flat.

The Reese's is super reliable; has high standards and doesn't like a lot of bumps in the road when it comes to life. He plays by the rules and believes in fairness. If I could use two words that would best sum up this guy……He's Safe!

For women who have made a lifetime of dealing with Twix's, Kit Kats, and Almond Joy's, this guy is a great find! He provides what none of those other guys do...a reliable track record. He calls from work to ask if you need anything at home. He doesn't leave you waiting or stand you up to hang with his boys.

You can bank on every word that he speaks. If he says he'll be there at 6:00PM, he's ringing your doorbell by 5:59.59PM.

The Reese's is practical and considers the BIG PICTURE. He is goal oriented, focused, and plans for the future accordingly.

He is the quintessential *"Family Guy"*. He's not interested in get rich quick schemes. In fact, he plans for everything. There are no surprises with this guy. What you see is what you get. He was made to marry and doesn't hesitate to pop the question when he feels the time is right.

The only problem with this guy ladies is that you may get a little bored with him if you have a spicier more adventurous side. His weekly trips to Walmart and Target may make you want to pull your eyes out if you don't share his very pragmatic view on life.

He's not a complete square. He'll wrinkle his shirt a bit at a buddie's bachelorette party or on special occasions, but he'll be sure to return to his regular scheduled program at the next given opportunity. He's a creature of habit.

He's the guy you can marry "Till death do you part" and be secure that he means just that, but he's not the guy whose vacation photos you want to be forced to watch at the family's fourth of July bar-b-que.

Every woman has dated a Reese's at least once in her life. In fact, he's the one that you find yourself running back to when your heart has been broken. He's often your relationship between relationships.

It blows my mind how many women pass over The Reese's. In fact, for a good part of my life, I was a Reese's. I realized after years of failed attempts of catching the "It girl", that they always seemed to go after the bad guy. So, I decided I had to become a bit more edgy and adventurous! It was a conscious decision and it paid off BIG!

I learned that women often confide in Reese's, but fall in love with The Twix's and Almond Joy's! As life continues and maturity sets in, their attraction shifts towards The Reese's.

I have a long-standing joke with my 65-year-old mother who is divorced and available: "When women are young and immature they marry for love, feelings, and passion. As they grow older, more mature and settled in life they marry for Social Security, 401K's, and benefits." LOL!

When women find solid, quality guys who are willing to provide them all the love and affection they desire and are able to provide a good living for them, they say he's boring! "Why?

I think it screams subconsciously," I don't believe I am really worthy of being treated like a queen. My self-esteem has been subjected to poor images and treatment and broken for so long, I don' t believe I am a queen. So, I struggle with your royal treatment, because I've become conditioned to my objectification."

Have you ever dated a Reese's? If so, write his/their names below:

_____

How did you feel in this relationship?

_____

_____

In your opinion, why didn't it work out?

_____

_____

_____

If the opportunity became available again, would you date him again? Why?

_____

_____

Do you honestly feel like you are and queen and deserve a man who loves you and treats you as such? If not, why?

_____

_____

_____

7. THE MILKY WAY BAR

The Milky Way bar is a chocolate- malt nougat covered with caramel and smothered with milk chocolate. The milk chocolate completely controls the expression of the other contents of the silky bar. He is a control freak. He will try to control every turn of your life. He will set all the rules for the relationship and you will follow them. Something about his tone and fear-filled words that make you punk right out and become spineless. You don't even see how ridiculous his rules are, such as the rule that you not go out with friends without him, or that you stop talking to your male friends, because they can't be trusted.

Once you're under his crazy spell it will be clear to your friends, family, and co-workers, but for some reason not to you. You'll feel great anxiety about ever speaking your mind or demanding anything from Mr. Milky Way. It's his way or no way at all.

He too like The Twix seems very regal and chivalrous in the beginning. He pays attention to everything that you like. He knows your favorite fragrance; the one that has always been successful at getting a man's nostrils to savor its gentle combination of florals and citrus. The one that got his attention. Lol. However, he suggests that you abandon that one to wear one that "he thinks" is more appropriate for a woman who is spoken for, because you wouldn't dare want to gain the attention of another man or ever be considered desirable by anyone other them him, right? WRONG. But, you ignore the warning signs because to you it's just great to have someone so madly in love with you that he's even a bit jealous.

If you allow his tyrannical behavior to go unchecked, he will control what you eat, what you wear, your diet, and how often you see your family.

His plan is to isolate you from everyone who has an ounce of influence in your life. He purges everyone from your surroundings who may voice their concerns about the inordinate amount of control he's flexing in your life.

You'll see all other relationships deteriorate one by one until there's no one left. When a man begins to pick out what clothes you should wear, it's no longer sweet, it's a sickness.

What causes a man's need to control of a woman? His control issues emanate from his feeling of helplessness or a lack of control in his own life. Controlling men attempt to control your life because they feel they have lost control of their own.

Have you ever dated a Milky Way? If so, write his/their names:

_____

How did you meet this guy?

_____

_____

_____

_____

How did you feel in this relationship?

_____

_____

_____

_____

Do you think a man's continual display of jealousy is an appropriate expression of his love for you? Why?

_____

_____

_____

_____

Have you ever lost your voice in a relationship to the point that you feared for your life? How did you get out?

_____

_____

_____

_____

_____

8. THE HERSHEY'S
"The great American chocolate bar!"

He is driven, clear and focused on what he wants. He wants to be the best at everything. He refuses to be distracted from achieving his goals.

This is a great guy to hang out with on occasion, but he may be one of the worst profiles to date, because he only cares about success and being the best.

He will be charming, and very engaging in his leisure time. He will appear to be what all the women want. Handsome, polite, and very courteous. He is a ton of fun to be around and is often recognized as the life of the party. He works hard and plays hard.

There is only one problem with the Hershey's. He's consumed with getting his slice of the proverbial American pie that on many occasions you will feel as though you are crowding his space and holding him back.
WARNING!!!!!!

Ladies, though his lifestyle is very appealing and you will often catch yourself envisioning yourself living in his home and riding shotgun in his foreign imports, YOU MAY NOT WANT

THIS GUY until he has reached the apex of his career. Even at this point tread carefully, because he is often prone to remind you of how you were made to be able to afford the lifestyle you experience and that fact that he did it!

He is the guy who will ask you to accompany him to a work function and spend his entire night ignoring you while he schmoozes with the corporate higher ups. He believes that is the cost of ascending through the ranks. Relationships are casualties of the success game he chooses to play. Women on his arm are usually arm candy, mere trophies and most often serve to support his image of success to bosses and colleagues.

He is a great breadwinner, but won't take the time to focus his efforts towards winning in a relationship.

If you can handle playing bridge with the old biddies, while he shares deals he's championed in the cigar room, then he's the guy for you. Not many women can handle this type of man, because you always feel like you're being cheated on. In fact, you are. He is married to his career and you are his full-time mistress!

He says I love you with Rolex and forgive me with a house full of roses, but will never emotionally invest in either experience. Emotions are something you do, not something you feel.

The Hershey's may have to experience multiple failed marriages before coming to the realization that: 1. He's not marriage material and should settle for casual dating or 2. His priorities need a total overhaul.

Have you ever dated a Hershey's? If so, write his/their names below:

_____

How did you feel in this relationship?

_____

_____

_____

How important is a man's career success to you?

_____

_____

_____

Some women don't require a great deal of maintenance in a relationship. Would a Hershey's be acceptable to you at this stage of your life/career?

_____

_____

_____

_____

*I believe that all women fit somewhere along the spectrum of three very distinct compatibility areas in marriage:

1. Wives (Emphasis on welfare of husband)

2. Mothers (Emphasis on welfare of children)

3. Partners (Emphasis on building a relationship where the husband is equally involved in parenting, as he is in being the breadwinner/earner for the family)

Where do you think you fit in this spectrum?

_____

_____

*This is very important to know when examining your partner's

compatibility.

9. MR. GOOD BAR

I'm nearly certain that you'll come across one guy in your lifetime and date him because *you should.* Everybody—your friends, your family, complete strangers—think this guy is perfect. He's handsome, he has a great job, he has a good sense of humor, he is kind, he is totally marriage and father material and he treats you like a queen. But again, the *umph* factor is missing. He doesn't excite you. You can have great conversations, but a certain inexplicable animal attraction just isn't there.

It will make you question, "What's wrong with me? He's perfect!" Well, that's just it. Perfect is boring. Wonk, wonk, wonk, wonk!

What I realized over the years of dating and failed relationships is that Women want a man that makes them feel secure and provides for the family; someone who wakes up with the kids and will help out around the house on occasion, but every now and again, they want to be made to feel like a woman.

There are times when John just won't do. They want Reqwaun, aka The Almond Joy. Women want a man to make them feel like a woman from time to time.

It's great to be needed, but it's necessary to be desired at times. Let's face it. The heart wants what the heart wants.

If you can work with your Mr. Good Bar and he's receptive to the training, (I hate to sound like he's a dog undergoing obedience class, but when you understand their best friends for a reason you'll be much more successful at dating and relationships) you can transform your Mr. Good Bar into what every woman really wants....

You must pay attention to all the details of the Mr. Good Bar. Remember, he's perfect on paper, but doesn't seem to add up in reality. There are a few possibilities at play here:

1. If you're interested in him, but he never seems to give you any play: Don't make excuses that he may be shy and you therefore, must make the first move and become the aggressor. Ridiculous. When a man wants a woman, even the biggest nerd will instinctively begin pursuit. Ladies please listen up here.

I've seen a lot of women get derailed in their thinking because a Mr. Good Bar was nice to them or paid for their meal. Mr. Good Bar's are nice guys, and let's face it. Nice guys do nice things, like open doors and carry friendly conversations. The truth of the matter is; He just might not be into you. Tough pill, but learn to swallow those.

2. He gives you real signs of interest, but you find yourself perplexed as to why you can't fully connect with him. It just might be something that you could have never imagined. Either you are a recovering "I Love Bad Boys"-addict or just maybe; instead of being filled with protein-rich peanuts, he might just be "fruit-filled" and for you that's a NO-WIN situation.

Lemme break this down for you nice and easy. If everything is right with your Mr. Good Bar. He finds an interest in you and you are a well-adjusted, "over your personal issues" kind of woman, but you're having issues connecting with him. He may not be emitting enough testosterone to get your hormones racing. Your Mr. Good Bar could be looking for a Mr. Good Bar of his own. Tough reality, but it's the world we now live in and I'm sure many of your closest friends have 'up close and personal' stories of this kind.

My advice to you, take a hard step away from this guy for a while until you can get your head in check. The worst thing you could do is think that you can change him. I've seen great women chase after what they thought was a Mr. Good Bar, but he wasn't showing signs of interest; only to find later that he had disqualifying desires. If you try to hold on thinking that he may see you differently, you might receive a curious roll in the hay, but you'll be setting yourself up for a massive let down, because you don't have what turns him on anatomically. Don't let it linger. It will only keep the fantasy alive. Walk away.

3. You haven't done your homework sufficiently on what makes him tick. When you speak to a man's interests, you captivate his mind.

Have you ever dated a Mr. Good Bar? If so, write his/their names below:

_____

How did you feel in this relationship?

_____

_____

Did this relationship lead to wedding nuptials?

_____

_____

_____

What would you diagnose as being the reason the relationship didn't work out?

_____

_____

_____

_____

10. SNICKERS
"SNICKERS SATISFIES YOU"!

The Snickers is *everything you've ever wanted in a man.* He's successful (as defined by his own sense of purpose), he's motivated, attentive to your needs, has a plan for life which includes you and creating beautiful little babies that look like the two of you. He is God-fearing and understands that his love for you is a reflection of God's love for him.

They key thing about the Snickers is that he's yours! While he will find other women beautiful and appealing; he understands that there is no one better suited for him than you. There will always be someone younger, smarter, even more beautiful, but they will never be you!

To the Snickers, your beauty is not beholden in the outward appearance alone. He loves your heart and the way you think. He's known from the day he met you that you were the one for him. He pursued you and you were excited to be found by him.

What is the secret to finding this Snickers? What does he look like, where does he shop for groceries? "Where can I find him?", you are probably asking!

My answer to you may be a bit perplexing, EVERYWHERE.

At the beginning of this section, I said that the Snickers is everything **YOU'VE** ever wanted in a man.

I can't tell you what he'll look like or sounds like or even where to find him exactly. The fact of the matter is that his traits and how he is in a relationship is less about him and more about you.

That's right ladies, you're Snickers is defined by your expectations of what you expect in a man! He may be fat, short, and bald or fit and tall with a head full of curly locks. You define who he is based upon your expectations.

YOU WILL NEVER FIND TRUE LOVE UNTIL YOU LEARN TO LOVE YOURSELF, TRULY.

One thing I know for sure. Your Snickers will aggressively pursue you, like a lion does a gazelle. You won't have to wonder if he wants you, because he will make sure that you know that he does. He's a predator and the affection of your heart is his targeted prey.

-He may not be rich, but his love teaches you to be satisfied with what you do have.

-He may not be supermodel fine, but he secures your mind in knowing that you are his heart, his love, his everything; which to you makes him more beautiful than Denzel and Fabio wrapped into one loin cloth.

-He may not be the best in the sack, but he makes love to your mind on the daily; and that makes his limited motion in the ocean, thrilling and orgasmic.

THE REALITY IS, IF A MAN CAN MAKE LOVE TO YOUR MIND, HE'LL KNOW HOW TO ROCK YOUR WORLD FOREVER! HE'LL HAVE YOU SCREAMING:

HELP! I'M IN A SUGAR COMA!

When you find your Snicker's he will make you feel you've found heaven on earth.

"HOW TO FIND HEAVEN ON EARTH"

Relationships are the spice of life. Everyone has a desire to be needed and a need to be wanted and will often find themselves doing the strangest things just to have "somebody" to come home to. Let's be honest and put it all on the table. We are all grown. I understand that your bed gets cold and lonely without biceps, triceps, legs, and thighs.

I'm sure many of you are tired of being lectured by the elders of your church telling you to hold on, God gone bless you with somebody just for you.... Well that's easier said than done, especially when she's taking her breast and thigh two-piece meal home to her dark chocolate drop.

Hold on ladies, don't throw in the towel. There is a way to find a chocolate bar so good that it will leave you in a sugar coma! If you play your cards right, you can have a bit of heaven on earth and it starts with YOU! Keep reading to find out what your man profile means.

"Understanding Your Man's Profile"

If I'm worth my salt as a writer and if this book is doing what I hoped it would, right now you should be asking yourself the following questions: "Which of these profiles does my man resemble?" or "Which of these profiles have I dated," and possibly trying to put a name to the profile.

Let's keep this in perspective: *It's all chocolate*! There were minor differences in the make-up of each of these candy bars, just as there are minor differences in the make-up of your man that may prevent him from or solidify him in becoming the man of your dreams. Only you can determine what those ingredients are and if they are a deal breaker.

The chocolate bar profiles were created to be fun and informative. Sometimes we are able to receive feedback more easily, when there's a bit of humor attached.

I would like to draw attention to a few profiles in particular: The Twix, Kit Kat, and The Almond Joy.
These three profiles WILL NOT CHANGE VERY MUCH. They have a tendency to remain the same from the cradle to the grave. Their resistance to change is usually tied to momma,

daddy and/or abuse issues that occurred during the developmental years of their lives.

They will show small signs of change for a season, but eventually revert to their misogynistic behavior in their relationships. Their lack of love, reason and empathy are often coping mechanisms for them to mask deeper seeded hurts rooted in pain and fear. Hurting people hurt people.

THE ONLY HOPE FOR REAL CHANGE for them is God, therapy, time, and for them to encounter a woman who is extremely secure and free of insecurities that will demand to be treated in the manner she deems acceptable.

WARNING!!!

If you are a woman with daddy issues, unresolved insecurities, abandonment issues, low self-esteem, or a sister who struggles with a "Captain Save a Bro" mentality; turn the page now and simply walk away. These men will have you locked in a cycle of craziness that will end with you being placed on prescription medication.

One of my favorite Disney movies is Beauty and the Beast. In this movie, the once charming prince had a spell cast on him that transformed him into this huge angry beast.

His only hope at regaining his true emotional and physical identity was to find a woman who would love him beyond his mean and evil ways. Along comes Belle. She was beautiful, strong and determined, and understood her real value. She challenged the beast to examine his ways and to treat her the way she desired to be treated. He fought her to remain the same, but she continued to challenge him, while uncovering and dealing with his emotional hurts.

The burly beast was changed into a gentle giant and became her Mr. Good Bar.

So, it's not entirely possible for these men to shift between profiles, but the work that it takes to get those changes underway are way above the average woman's pay grade.

THE REALITY IS, IF A MAN CAN MAKE LOVE TO YOUR

MIND, HE'LL KNOW HOW TO ROCK YOUR WORLD

FOREVER!

---

*The following chapters provide 9 Keys Women
Should Consider while preparing for Mr. Right!*

Please DO NOT turn to the next chapter until you have committed to yourself that you deserve the best. The best dating experiences, the best outcomes, and the best life possible!

Say this to yourself until it rings true in your heart:

I WANT THE BEST!

I DESERVE THE BEST!

I WILL RECEIVE THE BEST!

#1 KNOW WHO YOUR ARE

CHAPTER ONE
"Don't Get Lost in the Chocolate Sauce"

Great relationships are the product of two whole individuals who become one. Confident women, release a hormone into the atmosphere which attracts confident men. Just as insecurity in a woman is revealed before she ever opens her mouth to say hello. Insecure women don't realize it, but everyone can see their insecurities. It's often played out in how you dress, the way you act, the way you cling to any man in the room, and most often how easy she is offended.

YOU MUST KNOW WHO YOU ARE AS AN INDIVIDUAL, BEFORE YOU CAN SUCCESSFULLY BRING FULFILLMENT TO ANOTHER IN A RELATIONSHIP.

Never become so enthralled with the idea of being with a man that you begin to ignore who you are and the value you possess. This sounds like a no brainer, but I know scores of women who are so consumed with the idea of being in love with a particular man because he's so fine, that they've gotten lost in the chocolate sauce.

Therefore, I caution women to never date a man who you feel looks better than you. This reason is clear. If you feel he looks better than you, then he becomes the prize and you become the privileged. You begin to go out of your way to please him because he could have any woman he wants! If a man believes he can have any woman he wants, he usually attempts to do so. That's ridiculous. Buy yourself a TLC or Destiny Child's CD and listen to it on repeat, because you're suffering from a poor self-image. Male predators can smell that insecurity a mile away. This is why so many women find themselves devaluing themselves by hopping in bed with men that they never intended to sleep with. You were insecure and he spoke to your insecurities and made you feel beautiful, vibrant, and wanted.

This is a signature move of the Kit Kat and the Almond Joy. They prey on women's weaknesses. They tell them they are beautiful, perfect the way they are; using what male predators call the panty dropper line, "If you were my woman, I'd show you how amazing you really are." I've seen countless women fall for this bull hook, line, and sinker. (over and over and over again.) Please, heed the WARNING!!!!

WHEN A MAN SEEMS TOO GOOD TO BE TRUE. HE
USUALLY IS! HE'S LYING!

Put your goodies in time out. Here's a great way to see what his motivation is towards you: Take note of what eventually the conversation turns towards. If he continually turns the conversation towards your beautiful voluptuous curves, sexual innuendos, and/or even sex.... Run! He wants something you're not prepared to sacrifice. He either desires to take advantage of your finances or only wants your Scooby Snacks! Either way, he's using you to get what he wants.

*The Player/Lady Slayer*** behavior style:*

1. *Shows great affection to every woman around him.* 2. *Always looks you directly in your eyes while talking to you, as to be searching your soul. He allows his glances to linger so you know he's watching.*

3. *A bit touchy feely (doesn't overdo it) usually shoulders, arms, and hands.*

4. *Shows more concern than the average man about your feelings and listens very well. They usually target women who are lacking affection from their boyfriend or maybe their busy spouse.*

5. *Only acts this way in private, one-on-one, never in a public setting.*

The Wounded Warrior***behavior style:

1. *Shares with you a very deep emotional story about how they've been hurt in a previous relationship or about their neglect-filled childhood. Maybe of how he had to fend for himself and never was able to trust anyone, because no one has ever showed they cared.*

2. *When you catch them in negative behaviors, they'll always tell you they were never taught how to love or feel. No one ever took the time. It's just not what they do.*

3. *The purpose here is to have you feel sorry for them. They usually target "fixers"; women who think they can fix what's wrong with a man, because they think they understand them.*

4. *These men will usually have very little to offer. These are the guys who are gypsies. They never settle down, but plop from couch to couch, bed to bed. They will be looking to move in with you because they are always*

experiencing tough times. Don't expect this guy to help with bills, food, anything that displays responsibility.

They don't have anything and are okay with living from day to day. Why do they need anything when they can find women who will share what they have?

BEWARE!!

5. *This guy usually has a rotation of women on tap and is planning his next pit stop just in case you grow weary of his shenanigans.*

It would be extremely helpful if men came with a warning label: "Warning! This brother will promise you the world and give you the blues. He's broke as a joke and couldn't get a pack of Skittles on credit if he needed to. He will borrow your car, burn up your gas, and never think twice about giving you a penny!" Wouldn't that be helpful? Absolutely. Unfortunately, we don't, so it's important that we get to know ourselves extremely well.

WHEN YOU KNOW WHO YOU ARE, YOU WILL ATTRACT THOSE WHO ARE MOST LIKE YOU!

Guys who are beneath your dating criteria (and there should BE some guys that can NEVER earn a date with you) will never make it through the front door if you have clearly defined who you are, what you desire, how you're willing to be treated, and what you are willing to accept.

Before you enter into any kind of a relationship, especially a romantic one, you should be able to clearly answer these next questions:

1.   What is my value?
2.   Do I understand what I have to offer?
3.   What do I need to be satisfied?
4.   What am I willing to give of myself?
5.   What are my deal breakers?

When you do your self-discovery before you start dating, you don't have to call an audible. Be prepared so you don't find yourself compromising what you need or desire because you were put in a tough spot in the moment.

Audible 101: an audible is a football term: when the offensive team doesn't have enough time on the clock to huddle and wait for the coach to send in the next play, the quarterback has to call an audible. A play he calls based on the situations at hand.

Following are some common mistakes that women make when dealing with men. These are profiles that women often allow themselves to become:

THE BIG SISTER SYNDROME

This usually occurs when a woman likes a man, but the man doesn't quite feel the same way. She decides that she is going to be his big sister. This allows her the opportunity to stay connected with her love interest, hang out with him "no strings attached", and even receive affection, all under the disguise of being his big sister. However, she still likes him and is looking for a way to insert herself into his life. Silent heartache is your reward as he enters relationships with women *of interest to him.*

THE PURPLE HEART (HERO)

The Purple Heart Hero is the woman who will try to rescue the man that she desires. She provides assistance to him under the guise of "I'm just concerned about you. This is who I am, I'd do this for anybody." When in fact she wouldn't. She sees his affliction or need as an opportunity to get close to him and will go at strange lengths to do so, even if it includes lending him money. (NOOOOO!) However, he will use her kindness as long as she makes it available. He APPRECIATES you, but he doesn't LIKE you. The moment a better opportunity comes along, He's leaving on the midnight train to Georgia.

SURROGATE MOTHERS

She operates as a pseudo-mom toward a younger man. She recognizes that she is old enough to be his mother and uses that to her advantage, to hug, kiss, even caress the object of her desire. The reality of the situation is that she has fallen for this much younger man and feels weird in doing so. He may entertain your advances. He may be fully aware, but he is not interested in a relationship with you.

If the Surrogate Mother falls for an opportunist. He will tell her everything she wants to hear. He will give her all the affection and attention she needs, as long as she is providing the finances he needs. This is really a dark situation, because when resources become depleted, the relationship will be doomed for a heart-wrenching end.

FIXERS

Like the hero, you have fallen for a guy that you feel or maybe even know is not really interested in you. However, you think that you have the ability to fix what's wrong with him. You enter into a relationship with him that he exploits to the fullest and you use every excuse in the book to explain away his negative behavior. Deep on the inside of you, you know that you're in over your head, but there's a part of you that thinks that if you can get him to just see things differently and change his heart, he'll fall madly in love with you. You are so wrong! You may be able to get this guy, usually a Twix or Almond Joy, but you'll never be able to "fix" him. You can't fix what desires to remain broken. So, your heart ends up broken and your bank accounts empty.

#2 CLEARLY DEFINE RELATIONSHIPS

CHAPTER TWO
"IT IS, WHAT IT IS..."

When I first started dating in my early twenties, I randomly dated a variety of women, not having a clue as to the outcome of what each relationship would bring. There were some that I realized immediately had no chemistry. Others, I noticed were attracted to me more than I was attracted to them or vice-versa, and those who were inevitable to end up in the dreaded "Friend Zone".

In my mind, I knew how I was filing these women away and for some strange reason, I just assumed that the women felt the same way. However, I realized I had a problem as time passed on and the "friend-zoners" were responding to me romantically and the "no chemistry" daters were angry because I hadn't called them back. It became evident to me that these women were going out on dates with me expecting me to define our relationships. Tragic!

Ladies, you have a responsibility to define what each relationship in your life means and to be clear about what is expected.

Friend, Find or Fellowship

I would like to share a principle in dating I call **"Friend, Find or Fellowship"**. Understanding and adopting this principle in your life will help you to be more satisfied with the outcomes of your relationships.

When meeting new people for the first time I put them in the following categories based upon our initial meeting:

A Friend: Someone that I think I would be able to build a strong "strictly-platonic" relationship with that will be a great asset, listener, teammate or confidant.

A Find: Someone that I may have a romantic interest in. This person makes me feel interested in getting to know more about them on a deeper more personal level. They meet my criteria of wifey potential. (Never waste your time entertaining a relationship with someone who doesn't meet your marrying-type criteria. You're simply just wasting time.) Dating should have a purpose! Stop the speed dating! Every date should be an interview by which your ultimate goal is finding that special someone. Please listen, don't run brothers away with a bunch of talk about marriage. There is no faster way to get a brother to put on skates than to do that.

A Fellowship: This person is someone with whom I lack compatibility. They aren't bad per se, but we just don't click with one another. It's okay to say that, because you will encounter them. This person is someone that you will see every now and again whenever a group of friends hangs out. You don't talk on the phone, you don't even exchange numbers. Your cordial.

After defining to yourself which category these individuals fit in your life, you make it clear to them through your speech and actions. (This is where you begin to pay attention the body language and code words you may be using. You want to make sure that you don't lead guys on that are friend-zoner's and fellow shippers.

HERE'S SOME EXAMPLES OF WHAT IT MAY SOUND LIKE:

(friend) - "Hey you are going to be a really cool friend
     to hang out with at times."

(find) - "You know I really enjoyed spending time with you
     today. I look forward to getting to know you
     better."

(fellowship) - "Good meeting you. Had fun. See ya
around."

Once you've made these distinctions, it's important to put away your markers, because you may want to redraw the boundaries from time to time. But in most cases, your first response is often the most accurate. There will be some exceptions to the rule and you'll have to just play those by ear. BE CERTAIN that if you desire to redraw boundaries, that he is desirous of the same. Make no assumptions. Ask if conflicted. Here's how:

"Hey _____, It seems like we are really starting to hit it off. I didn't expect this to happen between us. Are you feeling the same way? I don't want to assume anything."

Avoid clinging on to people who are not interested in clinging to you. It's okay to wait and see if he calls you, before you rack up 30 outgoing calls to his phone. Can you say desperate? That kind of stuff is a BIG turnoff for guys.

The following note is for women over 25

If you think a guy is a "find", it's important for you to determine from him, which package interests him. Make No Assumptions:

1. Slow but steady open-ended friendship
2. A Great Date on occasion
3. Ms. Right potential

***Send the "Just a friend" to the Friend Zone and politely let the "chronic dater" know that you only date with a purpose. The last thing you need in your life is a guy who's addicted to dating you with no real thought of a future. DON'T WASTE YOUR TIME, unless your available for a really good concert or sporting event and would like the company. But don't get it twisted. He just wants to date you. That's the package he has chosen, so keep him there with no added benefits until he decides that he wants to upgrade to something more substantial.

Define your timeline: Now that you have the guy who would like to invest in the future, it's important that you spend time (not gazing into his eyes, the chemistry is already there), checking out deeper levels of compatibility. Does he want kids? What are his views on God? Does he have great relationships with his family, in particular his mother?

WARNING: 9 times out of 10. If a man has a bad relationship chronically with his mother, he'll quite often have a hard time forming intimate relationships with other women in his life!
Take this process nice and steady. Not too fast, not too slow. Enjoy this time together, but keep your ears and eyes open. You should be information gathering, not just being drug around for a good time. Most women become one of many because they aren't intentional at this point.

#3 Give Space for Grace

CHAPTER THREE
"What do You do When Your Dog Roams?"

Day after day in my office I see men and women who have been messing around. They lead secret lives, as they hide themselves from their relationships. They go through wrenching breakups, inflicting pain on everyone around them. They make desperate, tearful efforts to hold on to the shreds of a life they've betrayed.

They tell me they went through all of this for a quick thrill or a lust-filled moment of romance. Sometimes they tell me they don't remember making the decision that tore their life apart: "It just happened." Sometimes they don't even know they are being unfaithful. (I tell them: "If you don't know whether what you are doing is infidelity or not, ask your partner.")

From the outside looking in, it is insane. How could anyone risk everything they've labored to maintain in life for a few minutes of pleasure? It may seem completely ridiculous, but this sort of thing happens every day.

How do you rebound when Rover has roamed and been caught on someone else's lawn with his leg hiked up around a tree, but wants to come home?

YOU MUST LEND SPACE FOR GRACE

Even the Bible says that infidelity is grounds to release your philandering partner to greener pastures. But after your emotions have settled and the reality of starting over sets in, you may decide to give poor Rover a start over.

Reconciliation of broken trust is a very difficult and challenging process. But if both parties are committed to do whatever is necessary to make it work, it can result in a relationship of greater love and appreciation for one another than before the breach occurred.

If he is desirous of your forgiveness, complete transparency will be necessary for a period of time. This means accesses to his cell phone and records, daily calendar, and insight into each day's schedule. If he is not willing to provide these to you, then he values his secrecy more than his relationship. Accountability has to be at the center of these efforts.

Accountability: *Being where you say you are going to be, when you say you're going to be there. And communicating if there needs to be a change in plans, before you change them. Nothing more, nothing less.*

Never pursue restoration of breached trust if he is not willing to take the following steps. These are not optional, but a mandatory:

- Complete Transparency
- Acknowledge Actions
- Honesty
- Answer all questions no matter how difficult
- Listen to feelings
- Patience
- Own it (Take Responsibility)
- Over Communication

As you continue down this path it will become necessary at some point for you to simply, "let it go". You'll need to fight against the desire to ask more questions and bring it up whenever you get angry or something feels awry. However, NEVER turn in your spy kit!

When Mr. Good bar turns into a bad boy and is promising that his cheating ways are behind him, it's important to forgive him if you still love him. But I never recommend completely retiring your spy kit. Well, maybe you can retire your spy kit, but don't ignore your intuition.

It's always important to stay one step ahead of the game. Though it may seem counterproductive to trust, I encourage you to keep him on his toes and help him keep his head in the "NO Cheat" zone.

Here are a few non-threatening tips I suggest. I often hear my brothers say, these things keep them on their A-game:

- Casual unannounced visits to the workplace or jobsite for lunch, so getting lax is not an option
- Keep an eye out for new undergarments and new fragrances that you did not purchase. These changes highlight a new change in personal interest. It could be to spice up things for you, but it might just be to impress a side chick
- Inspect clothing before washing. Growing up I remember the wealth of information dirty clothes provided my mom. Just a tip, start with the rear pockets of the jeans.
- It's worth the trouble of being responsible for the cell phone bill, so agree to take on the responsibility of paying that household expense. You only need to be concerned with calls 8 min or longer.

There are many who will tell you if you're going to trust him than you should just blindly trust him.

There is no such thing as blind trust. Faith is the substance of things hoped for. It is the evidence of things not seen, and that's all your looking for evidence.

I only advise taking an occasional look for those who can keep your mouths shut. You can't give up everything you find, every time you find it, by arguing and creating a hostile home environment. The information you find could lead to the wrong conclusions. Just be observant.

If you are a woman who is always arguing and complaining, you are going to be very lonely. Because after a long day's work, a man only wants a place that he can find peace. Never disturb the peace in your home with unsubstantiated accusations.

Ultimately, you should only be in relationships where you feel secure. You should be looking to better yourself, and not have time for spying. That's an ideal situation. That you feel secure and never have to spy, but when trust is broken, it takes a while to get your swag back. Take your time and don't rush the process.

#4 MONITOR YOUR PROGRESS

CHAPTER FOUR
"Time is of the Essence"

The most important commodity that you have is your time. It is the only thing that you cannot regain or reproduced. So, it's important that you don't allow anyone to waste yours. You can get more money, but you can't get wasted time back.

I said at the beginning of the book that it's important to be clear about what's important to you and what you expect from each relationship. As time passes by this becomes even more important.

For some reason, a great deal of men, especially African American men, suffer from commitment phobias. We struggle with the idea of saying that we want to be with one woman for the rest of our lives.
I know that I will receive a lot of flak for saying that, but over the years I've seen my white counterparts get married by the age of 22 and my black brothers attempt to break world records for the longest engagement.

Don't become the chronic girlfriend. You must set standards and relative time frames for your relationship. You should be appalled that he thinks it's okay to date you for 5 years with no formal plan of consummating your relationship with wedding nuptials. Make it very clear to your significant other that you only date with a purpose!

When a contractor erects a new building, he takes extra time to ensure the integrity of its foundation. He knows what I wish more women would begin to understand. The foundation of any institution is most important. In the foundation lies the code that gives clarity to what the expectations are for how tall or grand the structure is intended to be.

This proves true for dating and relationships. The more stable the foundation the more stable the future is proven to be.

When is your Ribbon Cutting Ceremony?

Every new construction goes through a series of challenges before its completion. The structure is set firmly in place, then the walls and the windows; eventually the finishing touches of the structure are completed. At the completion of every new construction the owners plan a ribbon cutting ceremony to celebrate that the building concept has become a reality and it is firmly committed to future growth and activity.

Women you need to keep your man aware that you expect a ribbon cutting ceremony to celebrate your plans for future growth. If there is no plan for such an event, he may not be the one you've been hoping he'd be.

Any man that loves you will want to make you his own and let the world know that he has no interest in any another woman. A Ribbon cutting ceremony puts the nail in the coffin of his little black book.

#5 CONTROL YOUR EMOTIONS

CHAPTER FIVE
"Love, Lust & Loneliness"

On September 11, 1993 New York City's World Trade Center Towers were bombed, using commercial aircrafts that had been hijacked. It was the deadliest account of terrorism on US soil. Thousands of civilians and public servants were killed in the attack. Our nation stood paralyzed with fear, wondering what was going on. Were we at war? Are we being attacked on all fronts? The nation waited to hear from our Commander in Chief, with great anticipation.

Our sitting president, George W. Bush, told the world that Iraqi President, Saddam Hussein, was the responsible party for the tragic loss of life. So, America went to war, with an understanding that this new axis of evil was deadlier than any other because they possessed WMD's (Weapons of Mass Destruction).

I'm sure you're asking yourself what does this brief burst of American history have to do with a book on relationships. Everything. You see, after a global investigation was done, Saddam murdered and removed from power, Iraqi government destroyed and taken over by US Troops; we didn't find any WMD's and the storyline that we were fed as a global community to enter into war was also not true. Here's what we learned: 1. Saddam was not the perpetrator of the World Trade Center Attack, but rather Osama Ben Laden 2. There were no "Biological Warfare" WMD's in Iraq's possession.

The Weapon of Mass Destruction in play here was revenge. Wow! It was reported that Jr. Bush had learned of an attempt that Suddam Hussein had made on his father's life decades earlier. He wanted revenge! His emotions got the best of him and his Presidency and his political standing were forever marred because he allowed his emotions to run amuck and push him to do things that were in fact illegal and unethical.

Ladies, it is extremely important that you get your emotions in check, because they have the potential to wreak havoc in your world and on those around you. Unchecked emotions are the world's most dangerous WMD's! Come on I get chocolate is often so sweet and delicious that you may at times lose all sense and sensibility once you get a good dose of it, but NEVER LOSE CONTROL!

Lust, Love & Loneliness

These are powerful emotions. What are they and why are they so dangerous?

Lust is an unbridled desire to feed the soul what the soul wants. The soul is that part of your make-up that houses your desires. It's responsible for the chocolate cravings your body experiences and is so in synch with your mind that it's virtually impossible to know where one starts and the other begins.

If lust were a movie, your mind would be the projector that it's played on. It's an aggressive soldier that desires to march to the beat of its own drum; and so powerful that countless Godly men have fallen prey to its grasp and disobeyed God for its pleasures.

Lust shows addictive characteristics like a drug. It's wakes you up in the morning, will put you to sleep at night and will have you up driving the streets in the wee hours of the morning trying to extinguish its flames once sparked.

Many women find themselves in long term toxic relationships because they fell in lust with the wrong man. I find it amazing and quite ironic how many women choose their favorite chocolate bars. Most of the tools they use are all external and superficial: Is he fine? Is he paid? What does he drive? Can he lay pipe? And is he interested? Then you're amazed when the relationship fizzles due to a lack of compatibility.

IF YOU DON'T FIND COMPATIBILITY BEFORE YOU HIT THE SACK, THE SACK WILL BE YOUR ONLY AREA OF COMPATIBILITY.

That's why the best times of your relationship are when you break up to make up. So powerful are the moments that they've written several songs about it. This is a lust-driven relationship. My prayer is that all women would fall in love with themselves enough to make him wait until after the marriage, because sex confuses even the most confident woman.

How do you know if you've fallen in lust? Here are few questions you need to ask yourself:
1. Did I meet him at the club, bar or hang out spot?
2. Did I give him my attention or did he have to gain it?
3. Were his looks one of the main reasons you decided to date?

4. If you are sexually active. Is his man tool or sexual prowess the reason you keep coming back, even when you know it should be over?

5. Do you have to deal with baby mama drama and side chicks on the regular?

6. Do you miss his conversation when he's away for an extended period of time?

7. Are you uncertain much of the time where you stand in the relationship?

If you answered yes to any of these questions, it is very likely that you fell in lust with the chocolate sauce. These questions provide some very powerful feedback on the nature of your relationship and its core motivators. Core motivators are the key factors that keep people together. What is your motivation for staying? You'd be surprised how many women stay in relationships, just to keep their man away from someone she thinks he really wants.

The girlfriend:
-She sees the animal attraction that exists between the two of them. -She recognizes that there is something that connects the two of them.

-She's insecure whenever she's around. *(The other chick knows this by the way. Jealousy is like fried chicken on Sunday, you can smell it and know what it is right away)*
-She sees his interest in her and the sly "side-looks" he takes when he thinks she's not looking.

So, what does she do? She tries harder to keep the relationship together, when she KNOWS, she's not the object of his affection. This is one of his ways of saying, "I lust you, baby". Read the warning signs. Men are always going to look at a pretty woman, but his glances should never be read as disrespectful or "open" to further attempts of communication.

Love is patient, Love is kind, Love suffers long, Love is not vain, it doesn't blow up at you or brag of its intentions. Love is never having to worry about where you stand in a relationship.

When a man is in lust with you; he'll play mind games and may often want you to think he's cheating to spark up jealousy in you or better yet won't care if you think he is.

When a man loves you, he wants your world to be at ease and will do anything humanly possible to let you know that you are his one and only. If a man is more concerned with his privacy and security *(cell phone passwords, screen locks, phone calls that he has to step away or whisper)* than your sanity, he doesn't love you. He loves his secrecy.

I'm quite sure that many of the women who read this book have come to the conclusion that you're not sure if it's love or lust at this point. Here is a sure indication that he loves you, if you can say most these things are true in your relationship:

1. I always know where I stand with him.
2. He makes me feel like I'm the only woman in the world.
3. I feel secure in our relationship.
4. I don't <u>feel the need</u> to snoop, pry or spy
5. I trust him completely with my heart
6. He accepts me for who I am, not solely what I look like
7. He loves and appreciates the way I think
8. I have an equal voice in this relationship
9. When he's late, I'm concerned about his well-being, not whether he's been with someone else.
10. This feels like what I always believed love would feel like.

YOUR HEART WILL NEVER BE TRICKED

BY A FORGERY OF LOVE,
IT'S YOUR MIND
THAT SHOULD CONCERN YOU

Loneliness is a challenging feeling. We can be in a room full of people and yet feel lonely. It's a feeling that is often manifested when we focus on what we don't have over the things that we do. It creeps in when we are most vulnerable and has the ability to trick your mind into thinking a lust situation is actually love.

Many people, especially women will accept a counterfeit when loneliness arrives at their doorstep; when they would normally deny him before hello.

Loneliness attaches itself to things that bring comfort: chocolate, ice-cream, cake, and yes, the Tyrone's of your life. Have you ever wondered at the conclusion of a relationship, how you ever ended up with that person? It's because

LONELINESS ACCEPTS AS A POSSIBILITY WHAT REASON AND SOUND JUDGMENT WOULD RULE AN IMPOSSIBILITY!

The only way to overcome the perils and poor decisions it pushes you to make is to occupy your time. You would be better served spending an average evening with a friend at a movie, than to spend a wonderful night on the town with the date loneliness selected.

Check your emotions before making major decisions of the heart. Lust relationships bring chaos and frustration; whereas relationships grounded in true love speaks peace to troubled waters. You deserve to be loved. Mr. "Right-now" will never produce the joy that is guaranteed by Mr. Right!

#6 DON'T STOP MOVING!

CHAPTER 6
THE THRILL OF THE HUNT

Newtown's 1st Law of Motion (Law of Inertia) states: An object at rest will remain at rest and an object in motion continues in motion. So Ladies, Keep it Movin'.

I've said before and I'll say it again, Men are instinctually hunters. Hunters are invigorated by the thrill of the hunt. Lions prefer to take down their prey in a powerful head-to-head conquest. Only vultures like road kill (easy bait).

Women who are pursuing purpose and making moves are like gazelles on the open frontier. This is where the Kings of the Jungle come to hunt. This is not by any means an attempt to demean women, but there are certain animal-like behaviors that are consistent in humans since there is one divine designer.

There is nothing more attractive to a man than an independent woman. There is much to be desired about a woman who has her own. What many women don't realize is that many times when men look at them: "hair done, nails done, everything did" all we see a walking price tag. Don't get me wrong, we appreciate the effort and the energy it takes to look good, but in today's economy, the last thing a brother is looking to do is add more discretionary spending to his already stretched budget.

You might be surprised, despite discouragement from companies and colleagues, 20% of office romances are likely to end in marriage, that's second to 30% of relationships that start through the introduction of friends!

Listen to my logic here because statistics back me up: We spend the majority of our time at work in a given day that it's inevitable that you will form close relationships that have the perfect DNA to build a strong bond further down the line. Here's why:

1. Starting a relationship with someone in your workforce means you already have something in common, before you even get to know intimate details about one another.

2. Being in the same industry means you both are like minded and have similar interests.

3. Working in the same industry also means that at the end of the day, you won't have to struggle as many couples do to share the details of your day with a

partner who can't understand or just not interested in how your day goes.

Keep in mind the more often you are working, meeting, and networking, the more opportunities you have to be seen by men who share like passions. After all, where you meet matters.

WHERE YOU MOVE IMPACTS WHO MOVES AFTER YOU!

(Poll of Polls: Washington Post, Match.com, Meet.com)

Sitting at Home	ends with no Action
Moving in Bars	end in one night stands
Moving at Events (Concerts, etc)	ends in short term dating
Moving at Neighbors Events	10% end in marriage
Moving at Church	12% end in marriage
Moving at the Work Place	20% end in marriage
Moving through Friends	30% end in marriage

& Other Social Settings

The point of the matter is, if you want to be found, you must be *ACTIVE*! This is the perfect time to focus on you! Begin to work on your personal dreams and aspirations.

Don't sit at home being a needle in a haystack. You'll never be found. Get up! Get out! And get Moving with the gazelles. You'll find as you become consumed with the pursuit of a better you, your moving scent will cause you to find pursuers of your own.

#7 KNOW WHEN TO SAY WHEN

CHAPTER 7
BANKRUPTCY

When a company or an individual has exhausted all their options to remain viable, bankruptcy becomes the only solution. Bankruptcy is a serious situation and should be avoided if possible. It means that the company or individual's situation has become toxic and no longer able to provide what is necessary to function in a healthy manner.

The same is true of relationships. It is important to know when to say when. No relationship or individual should be maintained at the expense of your own sanity. It's time to make some tough decisions. Below is a list of the steps you must complete to determine if it's time for you to file chapter 7 on your relationship:

1. Analyze the insufficiencies of your Relationship

Every relationship *must be* a collaborative effort between two individuals that desire to grow together. In many dysfunctional relationships, you will find one individual working overtime to keep the relationship together and the other individual putting in minimal or no effort.

It is important that you take note of what are your deal breakers; the things that you are not willing to compromise for the sake of the pair. I've heard many people say they were willing to do anything to keep their relationship alive. However, you must remember a relationship is a combination of two whole individuals. If you have to give everything that you are to be with someone; you become the casualty.

Men often expect women to be the ones to make crucial sacrifices as it comes to time and effort. I'm not saying it's right, but it is how our society has evolved. But, beautiful ladies, a man who is both mature, secure, and accomplished will never want you to compromise your vision and goals, because he understands they are a key part of what makes you, uniquely you. Your thoughts and opinions matter, and he would never ask you to sacrifice more than he's willing to sacrifice. As a matter of fact, if he truly loves you, he'll become a sacrifice for you, because your dreams fulfilled is his heart's desire. Clearly identify if there are things that make your relationship toxic?

_____

_____

_____

_____

_____

_____

_____

_____

_____

2. Determine your redeemable qualities.

In most cases, just as there are very toxic aspects to a relationship, there are also qualities that make the relationship worth striving to keep it together. What parts of your relationship provide hope for a better tomorrow?

_____

_____

_____

_____

_____

_____

_____

3. Make sure you are eligible!

Just as filing Chapter 7 requires you to meet eligibility guidelines, so is the same with relationships. Does your relationship qualify you for bankruptcy? Here's why:

One day I received a phone call from a friend crying and broken about the demise of her marriage. This was a couple that I thought was iron clad. There were some issues that arose within the confines of the marriage that caused both parties to run to their opposing corners. Infidelity, lying, and broken trust were all factors. I received the call on a Saturday and the divorce would be final within a couple business days. The philandering spouse was seeking to come back home and try again. However, she was done, heartbroken, wounded, and emotionally bankrupt and at a loss of what to do next. The individual was bankrupt, but it didn't mean that the relationship was bankrupt.

What makes you eligible to close this chapter and file bankruptcy? Be honest:

_____

_____

_____

_____

_____

NEVER MAKE IMPORTANT DECISIONS
WHEN YOU'RE EMOTIONAL.
YOU'LL MAKE THE WRONG DECISION EVERY TIME.

I asked a simple question "Are you still in love with your spouse?" I directed not to respond to me, but to respond accordingly to their spouse through their actions after a week had passed.

I instructed them to make a list of everything great in the relationship worth saving and everything toxic during that 7-day period. In essence I was asking, "Do you qualify to file for bankruptcy?

I am pleased to say, that a couple weeks before the completion of this book, they had gone through counseling, restored the marriage, and rekindled their love for one another! Bankruptcy denied.

We become bankrupt as individuals when we pour all of ourselves into someone else's pool of happiness. A relationship becomes bankrupt when both parties have nothing left to pour. What do you do when the wine runs out of your relationship? If it's not completely over, you find more grapes and get in the press.

4. Redeem or reaffirm what's worth keeping.

If you find something significant worth saving, you'll BOTH need to make an investment toward keeping what's salvable.

Everything is not always included in a bankruptcy. There are some things that you have the option of not including. During the downward spiral of the relationship, one or both of you may realize that you haven't fought hard enough and have thrown in the towel to soon due to your emotions.

Many of you may find that you were better off friends than lovers. This often happens when we redraw the lines of those categories we spoke about earlier.

We've all thought once or twice, "We're such amazing friends, I'm sure we'd be good together so let's just give it a try!" That's why I caution you greatly before shifting the men in your life from category to category. Your spirit knows what best. Leave well enough alone.

What is worth redeeming, if anything?

_____

_____

_____

_____

_____

_____

Fill out the bankruptcy forms.

If you come to the conclusion that you have nothing left to give and the relationship is toxic, it's time to fill out the forms and declare Chapter 7. Sign on the line below.

X
_____

Remember that working through this process takes several years to clearly clear your record. The worst thing you could do is to abort this process by starting a "rebound relationship".

When you leave a toxic relationship, chances are there parts of your life that have become toxic as well.

So, do yourself and every man that comes in your path a favor. Remain single for a minimum of 6 moths so that you can release all of the baggage from the previous relationship. For some, this may take years, depending on how toxic the relationship was when it finally ended.

#8 FIND A MALE FRIEND YOU CAN TRUST TO   GIVE YOU THE REAL LOW DOWN

CHAPTER 8
BIG BROTHER'S Q & A

(These are real questions received via Facebook conversations from women on dating and relationship. I sure this will help.)

Q: **How do I know if a guy is interested in me?**

A: *Simple, when he tells you. No sooner. Don't be the woman who mistakes every kind gesture a man does for you as an attempt to win your affections. You will save yourself a great deal of heartache and embarrassment.*

Q: **How long do I wait before I introduced someone I'm dating to my child(ren)?**

A: *First ladies, please don't keep your kids a secret, thinking that you will scare him off. Actually, this is an excellent way to determine his level of commitment and sincerity with you. Any well-adjusted man (which I wasn't until my late 30's) will not have a problem with your children, if he's truly interested in you.*

Secondly, you are in the dating process, not your children. You should never introduce your children until you are absolutely certain that the relationship is viable for a long term commitment. I personally think it should be the last step of your dating process. After the parents and close friends have given you their careful consideration of a guy (and he passes!!!), then you can introduce him to your children as your friend.

***And please don't have your kids calling this man daddy until you, "say I do", because he still has time to say, "I don't. Our children have enough challenges to face, without becoming casualties of your dating disasters. What happens if it doesn't work out? Don't put them through it!

Q: **What do I do? We went on a date and I thought we had a good time. I haven't heard from him since. It's been three days.**

A: It's time for a reality check. Maybe the date didn't go *as well as you thought. Please don't become Dr. Phil and create an excuse why he hasn't called. If he felt   the date went as well as you did, he would have called you that evening to check on you. Certainly the following day. Remember, "Men don't like to hunted, hinted, and certainly not haunted. LET IT GO! If work kept him busy with a special project, you'll be the first on his call list the moment he free us, saying the same. If not, chalk it up to a nice time, but ask a male friend his thoughts. (Not a gay male friend. This is a need for a well adjusted heterosexual response. And they do differ.) I never understood why women ask other women what they think, like her response is going to be much different from yours. There may things that you are taking out of context or just plain missing.*

Q: Where should I be going to meet guys?

Nowhere. You shouldn't be going to place to meet guys. You should be going places to enjoy yourself! Humans release pheromones. Fun pheromones receive a different response than, "I'm desperate come get me now pheromones!" Remember Keep moving, he'll find you.

Now I think that it's cool to frequent places where men are prevalent, like Buffalo Wild Wings on game nights. Please make sure that you know the culture of the place you plan to attend. Hint: nails, hair, and Gucci bags scream PRICE TAG AND WORK! (Men love beautiful women, but they love natural beauty more. Some women go overboard with their beauty regimen and it's a huge turnoff, because it's too costly and takes too much time. No man wants to think that eventually he may have to wait hours for you to morph from shabby to chic, just to go out for a nice dinner.) You may get attention, because let's face it. We are men, but you would be better received and asked to join the group if you rockin' jeans, team apparel, a baseball cap, and you can keep the heels. We love those heels. This way you send message, "I'm a lady, but I'm cool to hang out with the fellas from time to time and just have a good time." Just try it. Results are empowering.

Q: **How do I know if he's cheating on me?**

Well, you won't KNOW that he's cheating until you catch him. However, if you feel like he's cheating. He usually is, or at least setting it up. (That answer is only for women who are well adjusted and not suffering from insecurities of a previous cheating mate.)

Understand this, men are creatures of habit. Study our patterns and note when we suddenly deviate from those patterns.

1. We take the same way home

2. We get home about the same time usually. When he starts having to "work late" all of a sudden, pay keen attention to other behaviors; that's the #1 excuse of most cheaters.

3. We hang out with the same group of friends.

Know your man and pay attention to his routines.

DO NOT! I REPEAT, DO NOT accuse your partner of cheating until you receive hard evidence. Because the moment you disturb the peace in your home (which is what we all want when we get home from a long day's work) he will leave. He's been beat up all day at work by the demands of life. The last thing he wants is to be beat up by the one person who promised to love him unconditionally. Even a great man will begin avoiding home. If he's avoiding home, he has more time to roam. Someone will see him out alone and give him all the attention he craves, knowing he's your man.

Q: **Why am I always attracting the wrong type of guys?**

A: *I hear a lot of women ask this question quite often. the answer is really quite simple. You catch what you bait for. A good fisherman knows that the most important thing   necessary to catch the type of fish that you're interested in   catching is the bait that you use.*

If you have taken inventory of your self esteem and determine that you aren't suffering from low self-esteem or a poor self-image, then this may be helpful.

The 3 most important rules of real estate are: Location! Location!   Location! You may find that you are not necessary attracting the wrong guys, but attracting what's in the pond you've been fishing in.   Fish are going to bite it the hook has bait.

If you're trying to send your kids to a school that has top teachers and excellent academic curriculums, you're not going to spend very much time searching for houses in low income communities.   Let's face it the money never lands far from the source.   Just as good, productive men are always found in places of high achievement or productivity.

Try shifting your waterholes.   Use your bait at a country club or golf outing, the Chamber of commerce business

brunch, or   maybe   even   save   up   your   money   to
splurge at a   fancy   restaurant.   Where you cast your
bait is just as   important as the bait you use.

Q: **I just broke up with my boyfriend a few weeks ago, and I just met the absolute best guy ever at my gym. What should I do?**

A: *Be honest with him and let him know that you just   got out of a relationship and that you'd appreciate if he'd give you some time to debrief.*

After an extended relationship comes to an end it is vitally important to any future beau that you take about six months and detox from that previous relationship. If you never unpack the baggage from the previous relationship, you will just wheel it right into the next one and begin unpacking it there. Before you know it the new relationship will have all the symptoms of the last relationship. Love yourself enough to regain yourself.

Q: **I just started dating this new guy and he told me that he and his ex are best friends. What should I think about this?**

A: *Take a deep breath and take it easy. This could be a good sign for you. That fact that his relationships end in an amicable manner, may in fact be a sign of his maturity and honesty in a relationship. Should she become his "bestie" or confidant in tough times. I think you should be honest that it makes you feel uncomfortable. He shouldn't have to abandon his friends (neither should you) as long as they understand the boundaries and don't cross them, but any friend that crosses the friendship boundaries has to be let go.*

However, at the same time, his ex should seem like his ex to you and everyone else. If he and his ex still have keys to each other's home or apartments, they still chat it up on the phone and hang out on lunch dates, they aren't ex's. They're still dating. Let him know someone's gotta break up. Him and his ex or the two of you.

#9 KNOW YOUR WORTH

(My purpose for writing this book is to help every woman understand that you are fearfully and wonderfully made. God created you with a purpose. You were not a mistake, but He was intentional in your design. Every strand of hair on your head, every curve of your body, every love handle, Big nose, wide eyes, skinny, fat, short or tall, you were intentionally designed by God. Embrace your uniqueness, because he has and he loves you just the way you are. So, on the next page I've taken the liberty to write you a letter. A love letter of sorts. Write your name in the blank space. Cut it out and put it in a frame. Allow it to be an example of what your Snicker should say and feel about you.)

CHAPTER 9

THE LOVE LETTER

Dear _____,

I know you're probably wondering why I've given you this letter. Put your heart at ease. Everything is okay. In fact, that's the reason I wrote you this letter. Because everything has been so perfect that I want you to know how I feel from the depths of my soul. From the very moment I laid eyes on you, something leaped deep inside of me and I knew I had to meet you. I remember that day like it was yesterday. Feb. 14, 2017, I often play it repeatedly in my mind, because it was the day that I finally learned the meaning of true love.

You hear people say there's no such thing as love at first sight, but my heart begs to differ. When you shook my hand, and gazed into my eyes I could feel my heart flutter; sputtering recklessly like a 16-year-old boy receiving his first kiss on the cheek from his grade school crush. You took my breath away. And I've never recovered. You've left me gasping for more of you, longing to smell the scent of your fragrance that hugs the long of your neck and radiates beautifully sweet florals and with a hint of jasmine.

I've struggled for hours just trying to figure how to start this letter. Should I say hi, good-evening or hello? You are such a remarkable woman and I need you to know it. Because of you, I'm a better man.

I feel the need to apologize to you for every man who's every hurt you, disappointed you or made you cry. I apologize because they didn't understand that their actions were robbing you of your life force. You will never have to worry about me intentionally hurting you. If I ever do anything to hurt you, please tell me. My only desire is to love you and give you the world.

All my life I've secretly desired to have someone who would love me for me. You've shown me a love that I never knew existed. You've loved me to life! My days have more meaning; they're more colorful, because each one is energized with the hope of seeing your gorgeous face. You are beautiful, intelligent, sexy, God-fearing, thoughtful, funny, courageous, and most of all, you're mine.

It's amazing how being with you makes me feel like superman, but your love brings me to my knees like kryptonite. You complete me in ways that I never knew I needed. You are my angel, my boo-bear (lol), my true love. My solemn prayer is that God grant me the strength and the wisdom to do everything in my power to not only make you feel amazing, but be amazing. I love you more than life itself.

xxooxxoo
Your chocolate bar

Special Thanks

This book is dedicated to all the women around the world who are putting in the work and making great things happen. To the women who love us, when we haven't been worthy of the love you've given.

RIH granny, Voncile Bowen. Life has not been the same since you went away. Thank you for your legacy of love and faith. You made me feel like I could do anything. I miss you so much.

To Geraldine M. Walker, my mother, my queen. I love you and thank you for teaching me how to treat a woman. Thank you for your love and support and believing in me when I often struggled to believe in myself.

To the Bowen girls and my aunts and second mothers Pat, Elaine, Dot, and Stacey. Thank you for correcting me, when I didn't treat women the way I should have. Your correction was an amazing display of your love. Thank you

To the most amazing step-mother any boy could find Mama San (Sandra McGlothin). Words can't express how amazing I truly believe you to be. You didn't accept me, you made me a part of your family.

Barb Littles you were the reason for this book. Your conversations challenge me to be better. Your intellect inspires me to dream a really big dream. Thank you

Candis Thomas, Devetta McIntyre, Sandra Ware, and Briana Sharper your insight and perspectives provided the focus I needed to make this happen. You are a group of powerful women!

My daughters Taylor, Destiny, Janaya, and Katrina, you deserve Snickers and I'm going to make sure you get just that. Thank you, guys for all your hard work.

Thanks Katrina Murrell for the amazing cover! You are the best!

www.ingramcontent.com/pod-product-compliance
Lightning Source LLC
Chambersburg PA
CBHW071127250626

47159CB00006B/2156